D1493745

For Malachi and his mum, Hilary, with love. – L.R.

For my loving husband, Brandon. – A.H.

This book belongs to

_____

The illustrations in this book were created using pencils, watercolour
and gouache paint, finished with digital methods.

Kelpies is an imprint of Floris Books. First published in 2023 by Floris Books. Text © 2023 Lynne Rickards
Illustrations © 2023 Abigail Hookham. Lynne Rickards and Abigail Hookham assert their right under the
Copyright, Designs and Patents Act 1988 to be recognised as the Author and Illustrator
of this Work. All rights reserved. No part of this book may be reproduced without prior
permission of Floris Books, Edinburgh www.florisbooks.co.uk
British Library CIP Data available ISBN 978-178250-841-0
Printed in Poland through Hussar

FSC
www.fsc.org
MIX
Paper from
responsible sources
FSC® C167221

Floris Books supports sustainable forest
management by printing this book on
Forest Stewardship Council® certified paper

Maisie the Mountain Hare

Written by Lynne Rickards

Illustrated by Abigail Hookham

Picture Kelpies

High on a hillside all covered with heather,
two little mountain hares cuddled together.

Maisie and Archie were leverets still,
just recently born on this summery hill.

"Stay here," said Mum, "while I nibble outside.
The long grass and heather will help you to hide."

Mum left them dozing a while in their form,
hidden from danger, all cosy and warm.

Maisie and Archie woke up with a start!
The sun had gone down and the sky had grown dark.

"Mum!" they both squeaked when she joined them in bed.
They reached out and snuggled up close to be fed.

Now it was dark, it was safe to go out.
They played in the moonlight and zigzagged about.

"Peekaboo, Maisie," called Archie. "Surprise!"
"I saw you," his sister laughed. "I've got good eyes."

Maisie and Archie grew bigger each day,
and Maisie was tempted to go out and play…

She poked her nose out in the bright morning sun,
then thought, "Maybe one little trip would be fun."

"Archie," she whispered,
   "I'm going outside."
But Archie was worried.
   "Mum told us to hide!"

"Our fur keeps us hidden.
   We'll hide as we go."
And Maisie set off.
   Archie couldn't say no…

Maisie and Archie crept through the long grass,
peeked out at the blue sky and watched the clouds pass.

High overhead they saw birds flying over,
and down in the grass they found sweet-smelling clover.

"Look at those rocks,
    Archie – let's go and see.
I want to climb up," Maisie said.
    "Follow me!"

The rock Maisie stepped on
    was speckled and grey,
but both the hares jumped
    when the rock moved away!

"Ouch!" cried a young bird. "You stepped on my wing."
"Oh, goodness!" said Maisie. "I'm sorry – poor thing!"

"You're brilliant at hiding," said Archie, impressed.
"Our mum told us hiding is what *hares* do best."

Thomas the ptarmigan laughed. "Is that so?
A hide-and-seek game is the best way to know!"

Thomas hopped down and he covered his eyes.
"I'll do the counting – one, two, three, four, five…"

The two little hares zipped away out of sight.
Archie went left, and so Maisie went right.

She wriggled down deep in a nice grassy spot.
Then Thomas called, "Here I come, ready or not!"

Maisie was sure she could win this with ease,
as long as the flowers did not make her sneeze.

Thomas flew higher to look all around –
and soon saw a little white speck on the ground …

"Found you!" cried Thomas. "Your tail was the clue.
I saw a white fluffball and knew it was you."

"Hiding out here is quite hard," Maisie said.
"I think I'll try helping with seeking instead."

Meanwhile, young Archie had found a great place:
a rock with a crack that left just enough space.

He squeezed in the crevice and shoogled around,
then waited a very long time to be found …

Thomas and Maisie spent all that time seeking,
till Maisie caught sight of her twin brother peeking...

"There you are, Archie!" she cried with delight.
"We started to think we'd be searching all night."

Thomas gave Archie the Best Hider prize,
and Maisie Best Seeker, because of those eyes.

With the sun getting low, the three friends said goodbye.
"We've got to get home before Mum!" Maisie cried.

Chill winds were blowing, the days growing colder,
and Maisie and Archie were both getting older.

"We're looking all patchy," said Maisie one day.
"It makes hide-and-seek very tricky to play."

Thomas said, "Look –
  I've got white feathers too!"
Mum said, "In winter,
  that's what we all do.

"Soon, snow will cover the
  whole mountainside.
So when we turn white,
  that will help us to hide."

Now Maisie and Archie were easy to spot,
and had they seen one flake of snow? They had not.

Although they were bigger, and able to roam,
they couldn't go nibbling too far from home.

One morning, an eagle
flew high overhead.
"It's coming right for us!"
cried Maisie with dread.

"Quick!" Archie said.
"I know where we can hide."
And they ran for their lives
down the steep mountainside.

Archie ran straight for his old hiding place,
but would they still fit? Would there be enough space?

In they both squeezed – it was certainly tight!
But now they were safe, hidden well out of sight.

"Thank goodness you spotted that bird," Archie cried.
"Without your sharp eyes, we'd be breakfast," he sighed.

Maisie responded, "You played your part too.
Without this great hiding place, what would we do?"

Slowly they ventured out, sniffing the air.
The eagle was gone, but they'd had quite a scare.

Mum was so glad that the hares were all right.
"Oh, look – now it's snowing!" she cried with delight.

Sure enough, lots of big snowflakes appeared,
and the two little hares hopped in circles and cheered.

Soon their whole world would be snowy and white,
and the hares would be perfectly hidden from sight.

Now there was snow, they could finally play!
Thomas came often, and stayed the whole day.

Archie thought hiding in snow was great fun.
"Ready or not," Maisie called. "Here I come!"

Maisie soon spotted a small speck of red,
two little black ears and a fluffy white head.

"Here's Thomas, and now I've found Archie," she cried.
"You win!" Thomas laughed. "Now it's your turn to hide."

Two little mountain hares snuggled together,
warm in their form against cold, wintry weather.

White as the snow, they were tricky to see,
asleep on their hillside, now safe as can be.

Mountain Hares and Ptarmigans in Scotland

Mountain hares and ptarmigans (tar-mi-gans) live on moors and mountainsides in the Highlands of Scotland.

Hares sleep in sheltered spots on hillsides, known as forms.

Baby hares are called leverets (leh-ver-its).

In late spring and summer their grey-brown colouring helps mountain hares and ptarmigans blend in with heather and long grasses, keeping them hidden from predators, like stoats and golden eagles.

In autumn they gradually turn white to keep them camouflaged when it snows.

Due to climate change, snow often comes to the Highlands later in the year, and hares and ptarmigans sometimes turn white before there is any snow to hide them.